DATE DUE

SEP 21 '91	OCT 0 1 '92	NOV 14	
SEP 26 '91	FEB 0 2 '93	DEC 17	
	MAR 0 2 '93	JUN 13	
OCT 14 '91	OCT 21 '93		
OCT 31 '91	AUG 09 '94		
DEC 2 '91	WITHDRAWN		
JAN 6 '92	Jackson County Library		
JAN 13 '92	SURPLUS OR OBSOLETE		
FEB 04	JUN 29 '95		
FEB 19 '92	SEP 30 '95		
	MAR 14 1996		
MAR 4 '92	JUL 21 '97		
MAR 20 '92	NOV 06 97		
JUL 27 '92	APR 02 01		

GAYLORD   PRINTED IN U.S.A.

Grandfather's
LAIKA

This edition first published 1990 by Carolrhoda Books, Inc.
Originally published 1989 by Carlsen if-Bokforlag, Stockholm, Sweden, under the
title FARFARS LAJKA.

Text copyright © 1989 by Mats Wahl
Illustrations copyright © 1989 by Tord Nygren
English language rights arranged by Kerstin Kvint Literary and Co-Production
Agency, Stockholm, Sweden

LIBRARY OF CONGRESS CATALOGING-IN-PUBLICATION DATA

Wahl, Mats, 1945-
    [Farfars Lajka. English]
    Grandfather's Laika / Mats Wahl ; illustrations by Tord Nygren.
        p.   cm.
        Translation of: Farfars Lajka.
        Summary: Grandpa and his grandson Matthew share their worries and
overcome their grief together when Grandpa's dog becomes sick and dies.
        ISBN 0-87614-434-2 (lb. bdg.)
        [1. Death—Fiction. 2. Grandfathers—Fiction. 3. Dogs—Fiction.]
I. Nygren, Tord, 1936-   ill. II. Title.
PZ7.W12665Gr   1990
[E]—dc20   89-48619
                                                       CIP
                                                        AC

Manufactured in the United States of America

1 2 3 4 5 6 7 8 9 10 99 98 97 96 95 94 93 92 91 90

Grandfather's
LAIKA

by Mats Wahl · illustrated by Tord Nygren

Carolrhoda Books, Inc./Minneapolis

My name is Matthew. Every day after school, Grandpa waits for me outside of kindergarten. He's not allowed to come in because Laika is with him. Laika is a golden retriever, and she's very big and smart.

When I come running out of school, Laika barks. Molly stands inside the doorway because she's afraid of dogs. She doesn't have to be. Not of Laika, anyway. Laika is so kind and soft that it seems as if you could hide your face in her coat and disappear. As soon as I get outside, I hug Laika. Then I hug Grandpa, and we walk home together.

While we're walking, Laika runs along the edge of the woods. She sniffs everything and wags her tail all the time.

"See how yellow the birch tree is now?" asks Grandpa, pointing.

"Is it going to die?" I ask.

Grandpa shakes his head.

"No," he says. "It has just stopped sucking up water for its leaves. When they don't get any water, the leaves turn yellow and fall off."

"Why doesn't the tree suck up water anymore?"

"Because water freezes and turns to ice in the winter. If it becomes ice inside the birch, the tree could burst."

"But what about that tree over there?" I ask.

"That's a willow," says Grandpa. "It's not afraid of winter like the birch is. It stays green longer. Maybe it's foolhardy."

I try to figure out what foolhardy means. I don't ask. Some things I try to understand by myself.

And all the time, Laika is rushing around, sniffing everything.

When we get home, Laika gets her food in a bowl. She doesn't eat much. I'm glad that I'm not a dog because the food doesn't look very good. I eat two cheese sandwiches, and Grandpa makes hot chocolate for me.

When I'm through eating, I lie down on Grandpa's rug. It's in front of his sofa and has black and brown stripes. Laika lies down beside me, and I lean my head against her. With one hand I pet Laika, and with the other I feel the rug.

Once in a while, Grandpa tells me he's going to buy a new rug. "That one is so old," he says. But I ask him not to because I like the rug. I love lying on it beside Laika.

While I am resting, Grandpa sits in his chair. He asks me what I've been doing all day, and I climb up on his lap and tell him about a cave we made at school. Later he says it's time for a walk. "Before it gets too dark," he says as he looks out the window.

We put on our coats and go into the woods behind his house. It's a big woods beside a lake, and Laika runs in the trees and plays by the water. Now and then Grandpa calls her back to him. When we get home, it's dark and Grandpa turns on the lights.

At six o'clock Grandpa takes me to my house, and Mom and Dad are home when we get there. Laika wags her tail, and I give her and Grandpa a hug good-bye.

"See you tomorrow," says Grandpa.

It is raining the day Grandpa tells me that
Laika is sick. It rains and rains and rains and
is very dark. The wind blows against us as
we walk home from school, and it feels like
we might be swept up off the ground.

"The leaves will start blowing off the trees
now," says Grandpa. "When we get home,
we'll dry Laika off with a towel."

She is soaked through, just like after a
bath, and I dry her as much as I can. When
we lie on the rug, her coat is wet against
my neck.

Grandpa turns on the light next to his chair. "I have to tell you something," he says. "Laika is sick. I'm going to take her to the veterinarian on Friday."

"What's the matter with her?" I ask.

"She's stopped eating," says Grandpa. "She only drinks water. If you look closely at her, you can see that she's lost weight."

I sit up and pet her. "She isn't thinner," I say.

"Yes, she is," says Grandpa.

But I can't tell. To me she looks just the way she always has. "Maybe she does the same thing the birch trees do," I say.

"What do you mean?" asks Grandpa.

"Maybe she has stopped eating because winter is starting," I say. "Maybe she won't eat because it's getting colder."

Grandpa shakes his head. "I'm afraid she is sick," he says.

On Friday Grandpa goes to the veterinarian with Laika. On the way home from school, he tells me about the sick animals that were there. A cat, two dogs, a rabbit, and Laika.

"Has she started eating again?" I ask.

"No," says Grandpa, "she still won't eat."

"I think she's fatter," I say.

For a while, Grandpa says nothing. Then he says that Laika is not going to get better.

"But I'm sure she will," I say, looking at her as she sniffs a tin can in the grass.

"No," says Grandpa. "She's not going to. She's too old."

"She is foolhardy," I say.

Grandpa looks at me as if he doesn't understand what I mean.

"No," he tells me, "she isn't foolhardy, just old."

We are quiet the rest of the way home. I don't like it when Grandpa says something is old. Sometimes he says it about himself. "Old boy," he calls himself. That makes me mad. I don't like to hear that something is old. Grandma was old before she died.

While I'm lying on the rug with my head leaning against Laika, I ask Grandpa if she's going to die soon.

"Yes," says Grandpa.

I start to cry because it's sad when someone dies. Especially somebody you have leaned your head on and thrown sticks to.

"I'm going to the veterinarian with Laika again next week," says Grandpa. "She will get a special shot and fall asleep."

"Fall asleep?" I ask. "Do you mean she will die?"

"Yes," says Grandpa. "But she won't feel anything. It won't hurt her."

"Will her heart stop?" I ask.

"Yes," says Grandpa. "First she will close her eyes, and then her heart will stop."

"It's a very old heart," I say, feeling how it beats inside Laika under her coat. Later on, I sit on Grandpa's lap and cry for a while.

"Everything that lives must die sometime," Grandpa says.

I think about Laika and I'm sad.

"Are we going to bury her afterwards?" I ask.

"Yes, we'll bury her body," says Grandpa. "But we won't bury everything. Something important will be left behind."

"What's that?" I ask.

"The memory of how it feels to pet her," says Grandpa. "Your hand will remember how it felt."

I look at my hands.

"Can Laika remember us too?" I ask.

"It's hard to say," says Grandpa. "I don't know if you remember anything when you are dead."

"Will we put her body in a grave?" I ask. Grandpa nods his head.

"Her body will turn into dust," he says. "Everything will turn into dust."

"Tin cans don't," I say.

"No, not tin cans," says Grandpa. "Only things that were alive turn into dust. Tin cans are dead from the start."

"Nobody remembers a tin can," I say.

"I suppose not," says Grandpa, looking at me the way he sometimes does.

"Tin cans are foolhardy."

Grandpa laughs, and so do I.

Then one day Grandpa comes to pick me up from school, and Laika is not with him. I'm afraid, and I start to cry right away because I know she has died.

"Where is Laika's body?" I ask Grandpa while I'm lying in front of the sofa. I feel the rug with my hand. The rug still smells like Laika, but her bowl is gone from the kitchen.

"In the garage," says Grandpa. "I'm going to bury her tomorrow."

"I don't want to watch," I say.

Grandpa nods and says, "If you want to, we can see her grave another day."

I feel the rug and smell it and wonder if I will ever want to.

The next week we visit the grave. It's deep in the woods, near the lake where Laika used to swim. If you stand beside her grave, you can look out over the water.

"You picked a nice place," I tell Grandpa.

Laika's grave is under a birch tree, and some of its yellow leaves have fallen on the ground.

After we come back, I lie down on the rug and pat it with my hand. It still has Laika's smell. Soon I fall asleep.

"You can have the rug, if you want it," says Grandpa when I wake up. "I'm going to buy a new one." I would like to have it very much.

Grandpa calls my mom at work, and in the evening she drives over to get me and the rug.

After I unroll the rug in my room and lie down on it, I breathe in the smell. The smell of Laika is still there. Mom looks in from the doorway and asks me what I'm doing.

"I'm remembering Laika," I say.

"I see," she says.

Before I go to bed, I tell her not to vacuum the rug. I tell Dad too, and they promise they won't.

Later I ask Mom what "foolhardy" means, and she explains it to me.

The next day the ground is white with snow when I wake up. But the willows are still green, even after the first snow of winter.

I smile and say to myself, "Those foolhardy willows."